This book belongs to

....

Written by Elanor Best.
Illustrated by Lara Ede.

Taylor Tiptoe

Elanor Best • Lara Ede

make
believe
ideas

Tiny **Taylor** loved to *dance*: her **feet** would NEVER stop.

She'd **spin** and twist

and

Leap and *twirl*,

then

shimmy,

shake, and **hop**.

For this year's Summer Showcase, **Taylor** longed to get the *chance* to play the leading **princess** and **prove** that she could *dance*.

But every time poor **Taylor** tried to strike a perfect *pose*, no one seemed to notice in the sea of *pointed toes*.

In fact, she was so **LITTLE**

and so **very** hard to spot,

the other dancers *passed* right by

this tiny *tutu* dot!

"There's just **one** *dancer* who can **help:**

the magic
Queen Delphine."

So, on her tiptoes **Taylor** skipped along the *winding* street...

and **didn't** stop UNTIL she stood at **Delphine's** pointed **feet**.

"My only wish is to be tall," said **Taylor**, feeling **brave**.

"I can **help**," the *queen* replied,
and gave her wand a *wave*.

Sparkles

fizzled in the air,

around small **Taylor's** toes.

And then she *gasped*

as she began . . . .

and grow

...to grow

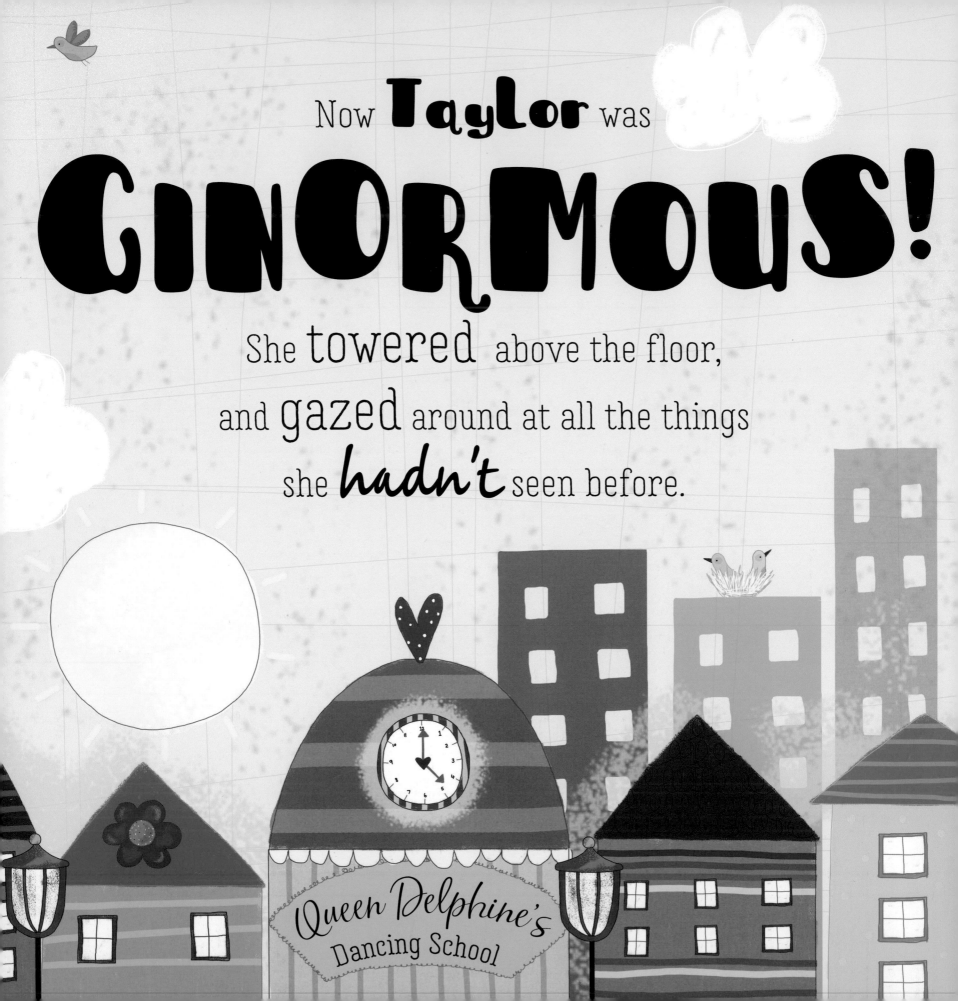

Now **Taylor** was

GINORMOUS!

She **towered** above the floor,
and **gazed** around at all the things
she **hadn't** seen before.

Queen Delphine's
Dancing School

But back at school, when **Taylor** danced, *everything* went wrong.

She couldn't keep her *balance* for her **Legs** were far too long.

Worst of all, now she was *tall*, she found she had to duck. She **couldn't** get through **any** door without first getting **stuck!**

Taylor rushed back to the **queen** to see what she could do.

"I've got a **plan**," wise **Delphine** said. "Now **try** just being **YOU!**"

"The secret to good *dancing* is **not** your looks or height. It's something *within* YOU that shines much **brighter** than the lights!"

Now **Taylor** knew just what to do
to get on with her mission.

She took a **breath**,
puffed up her chest . . .

and ran to the audition.

With **bravery**,
she *leapt* on stage
and **pointed** both her feet.

She *whirled* and whizzed
and bounced and *fizzed*

and **boogied**

to the **beat.**

Summer
SHOWCASE

starring
(the tiny but terrific...)

Taylor
Tiptoe

For one night only

Queen Delphine's Dancing School Auditorium

Tickets on the door

At last the Summer Showcase came,
and **Taylor** played her part.

She *danced* the best, despite her size,
for she danced with all her **heart!**

Taylor's wish had made her learn
the **one** thing that was **true:**
there's nothing that you **can't** achieve
if you *believe* in **YOU!**

Royal box

She *danced* the best, *despite* her size,
for she danced with all her **heart!**

Taylor's wish had made her learn
the **one** thing that was **true:**
there's nothing that you **can't** achieve
if you **believe** in **YOU!**

Royal box